Isadora Take That Thumb Out of Your Mouth!

Story by Avelynn Myers
Illustrations by Mirjana Bubevska

2

Isadora Diore was a mermaid.
She lived far, far away from land...
far out in the turquoise sea.

Isadora Diore had a habit.
A really bad habit.

You see...

Isadora Diore
always had her thumb
in her mouth!

Her mama would always say...

"Isadora!
Take that thumb
out of your mouth!"

But that did not help
and Isadora would forget.

And there were days it seemed
her habit just would not,
and could not, be broken.

Her thumb was in her mouth...

when she woke up in the morning.

while she brushed her hair.

Her thumb was in her mouth...

when she swam with
her friends to school.

Her thumb was in her mouth...

when she solved problems
during math class.

Her thumb was in her mouth...

when she painted during art.

when she did pirouettes at ballet.
And yes... mermaids can do ballet!

And at the end of every day,
her thumb was in her mouth...

as she fell fast asleep.

In fact,
her thumb was in her mouth...

ALL...
THE...
TIME!

And her mama would always say...

"Isadora!
Take that thumb
out of your mouth!"

But that did not help
and Isadora would forget.

And there were days it seemed her
habit just would not, and could not,
ever be broken!

Isadora listened to the dentist tell her how putting her thumb in her mouth could make her teeth crooked.

But she could not break her habit!

Isadora listened to the doctor tell her how her thumb can have all kinds of icky germs.

But she could not break her habit!

And Isadora did not like when the other mermaids teased her for it.

But she could not break her habit!

Isadora couldn't remember
why she started putting her thumb
In her mouth in the first place...

and try as she might,
she could not break her habit!

And so her mama would always say...

"Isadora!
Take that thumb
out of your mouth!"

But that did not help,
and Isadora would forget.
And there were days it seemed
that her habit
just would not,
and could not,
ever be broken!

Then one day,
Isadora's mama brought home a
special gift just for her.

A very special gift.

It was a pair of fancy, sparkly
mermaid gloves!

"They will remind you to
take that thumb
out of your mouth!"

Her mama told her there was
just one rule... she could not
take them off.

Isadora was so excited to
wear the fancy gloves!

They sparkled...
they glistened...
they were magnificent!

Isadora wore them to bed that night.
She admired her fancy gloves before
she fell fast asleep.

Her mama did not have to say...
"Isadora! Take that thumb
out of your mouth!"

She was still wearing them when she woke up. She admired her fancy gloves and got ready for the day.

Her mama did not have to say...
"Isadora! Take that thumb
out of your mouth!"

She wore them while she
brushed her hair.

Her mama did not have to say...
"Isadora! Take that thumb

She wore them as she swam to school.

She showed her friends her special
mermaid gloves.

They said "Oooh!" and "Aaah!"
They admired her fancy gloves.

In fact, they wanted a pair too!

She wore them during math class...

and solved all the problems!

But then, during Art, Isadora forgot.
She was about to put her thumb in
her mouth, when suddenly...

she saw her special glove and
stopped! Her mama was right...
they had a special power!

Isadora wore her gloves during her ballet class.

She did a proper pirouette with her hands raised high.

And that night, Isadora went to bed
with her gloves still on...
and fell fast asleep.

And her mama did not have to say...
"Isadora! Take that thumb
out of your mouth!"

Isadora woke up the next morning.

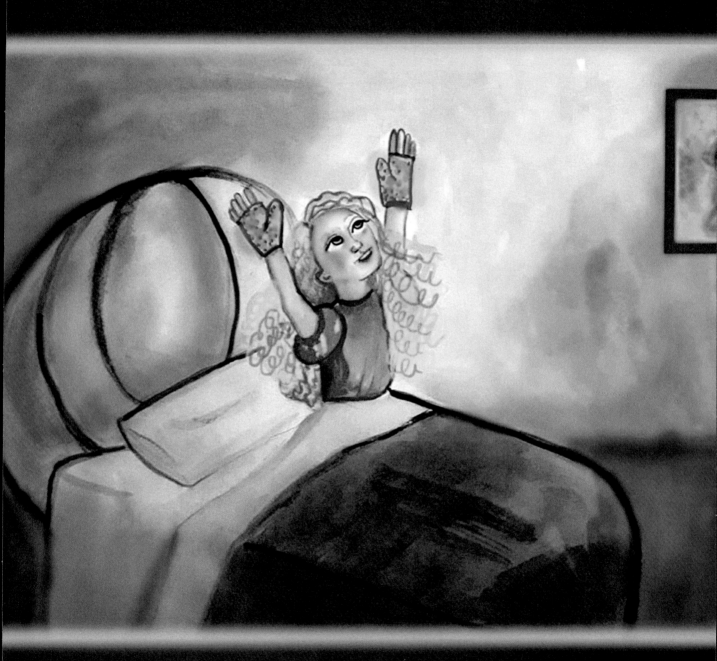

She stretched her hands up
high in the air.
She got ready for the day.

She admired her fancy gloves.

Today was a new day
to practice breaking her habit.

And Isadora Diore was excited to use her fun and sparkly reminder to...

keep that thumb
out of her mouth!

Before she left for school, Isadora
gave her mama a great, big hug.

Her mama whispered, "Be kind to
yourself... if you forget, you can
always try again."

But today Isadora was determined
to keep that thumb
out of her mouth!
Isadora hugged her mama tighter.

And so she did.

Now Isadora Diore was ready to
take on this brand new day.

37432455R00024